METTA'S BEDTIME

WRITTEN BY: METTA WORLD PEACE

WITH: HEDDRICK MCBRIDE

ILLUSTRATED BY: HH-PAX

EDITED BY: TILEA COLEMAN
AND
YOLONDA D. COLEMAN

ISBN: 0615700756

ISBN-13:978-0615700755

DEDICATION

Metta's Bedtime Stories is dedicated to ALL children, families, and educators. These stories were written to help children think about things that happen to them from day to day. Children will keep an open mind and learn a new lesson with each page. They will learn to accept good and bad days. This book will show readers how to have a better day tomorrow with a hopeful heart and positive thoughts.

Reach for the Sky

Reach for the sky, and your dreams can come true.
You can do anything you want to do.

You can be a doctor, lawyer, and a teacher too.
If you like animals, you can work at the zoo.

Reach for the sky, and you can be a movie star.
You can also become the driver of a fast race car.

You can be a firefighter, whether you are a boy or girl.
You can be the president who brings peace to the world.

You can be a singer, model, or a big time artist.
You can be the carpenter who works the hardest.

You can try your hardest at sports. You'll be a winner.
You can be a famous chef who makes the best dinner.

Never forget to do your best at anything you try.
As long as you keep reaching, you can make it to the sky.

I'm afraid of the dark. So what can I do?
I asked, "Mommy, Daddy, can I sleep with you?"

Mom said, "You can't sleep with us. You are getting too old.
I guess it's time for this story to be told."

When I was a little girl I was afraid of my chair.
When all the lights went out a monster sat there.

He never moved or made a sound; he kept watching me.
He let me run out of the room without stopping me.

Why did he only come to my room after dark?
I never saw him at school or when I played at the park.

One day we played for hours at the playground.
I was so tired; I couldn't wait to go home and sit down.

I quickly sat down on my favorite chair.
Then I noticed nothing was there.

It wasn't a monster standing tall.
It was simply a shadow on the wall.

It's normal to be afraid of things you don't know.
When you see things for yourself your courage will grow.

It is very important to stand up to your fears.
That shadow in the dark is not as big as it appears.

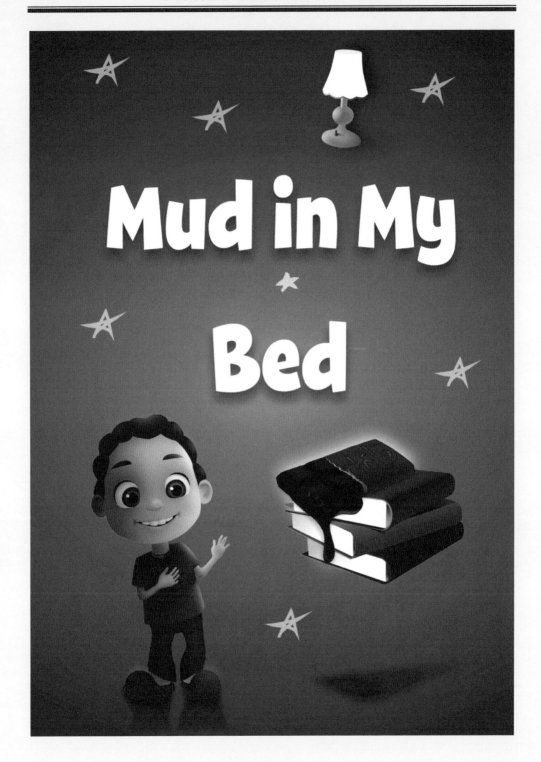

Mud in My Bed

When I woke up this morning and opened my eyes,
there was mud in my bed, to my surprise!

I ran to the bathroom to wash my hair out.
When I looked in the mirror I gave a little shout.

I stared and looked as I leaned over the sink.
Who would do something like this? I really had to think.

Maybe it was my brother; he is always playing.
"Nope, it wasn't me." That's all he kept saying.

The only suspects left were my Mom and Dad.
"No, it wasn't us." That's what they both said.

Dad said "Think about everything that you did yesterday.
Then you will find out how your hair ended up this way."

I was in my bed last night after my evening shower. Then I got hungry and needed a little snack power.

I went downstairs and grabbed a chocolate bar to eat. I must have fallen asleep before my snack was complete.

In the end I just shook my head.
I was the one who put the mud in my bed.

Tomorrow

Today was a good day, but tomorrow will be better.
You have to put all of the good thoughts you have together.

Today you learned a new word, and tomorrow you will know
two. Each day you will get better at everything you do.

You will have a chance to do the things that you love most.
Like having fun with family and holding them close.

Today was a bad day, and you made a few mistakes.
Tomorrow you will do better no matter what it takes.

You can control the next day, but you can't change the past.
You can do great things, and become the head of your class.

If you miss your friends, tomorrow you can see them.
When you have goals and dreams, then one day you will achieve them.

Saying goodbye to today should never cause sorrow.
Great things are waiting for you tomorrow.

One Wish

One day my friends and I were on the playground when a beautiful fairy appeared and said, "Kids gather around."

"There's a fairy who takes teeth and one who gives kisses.
I am different because I grant wishes.

Get in line to tell me what you would like to have.
Take your time and be polite. There's no need to push and grab."

Heaven went first, and she was as clear as could be.
"I wish that all blind people would be able to see."

Miguel wished for all the soldiers to return home without
harm. He heard that during the war some may have hurt a leg
or an arm.

Carol wished for the neighborhood to have safer streets.
Everyone would get along and there would be peace.

Hector wished for brighter lights to be near the park.
Everyone would be able to see after dark.

Vanessa wished for everyone to get the food they need.
If everyone had enough there would be no greed.

The fairy said, "Of all the kids that I've ever met, this is the group that has wished the best."

She said that since we all wished for things that involved others, we will become great leaders, teachers, fathers, and mothers.

"If you wish for good things to happen, your wishes will come true. Blessings and good fortune will always reach you."

Visit www.mcbridestories.com for more titles.

Made in the USA
Charleston, SC
03 July 2013